FAIRYTALE CLASSICS

Aladdin

Anna Bowles

Shahar Kober

LiTTLE TiGER

LONDON

Aladdin was a clever, cheeky boy who lived with his mother. One day a stranger knocked on their door.

"I'm your long-lost uncle," he said. "And I'm a magician. I have a job for you that will make us rich!"

Aladdin's mother didn't remember having a brother. But she was definitely fed up with being poor. So she let Aladdin go.

"We're going to find a precious lamp!" said the magician.

In a cave?

Be quiet. And start crawling!

Aladdin
squirmed
through tiny
tunnels. Soon he
saw a golden lamp.

"Give it to me!"
bellowed the
magician. But the lamp
was so beautiful Aladdin
wanted to keep it. The
angry magician blocked
the cave entrance. There
was no escape!

Aladdin hugged the lamp tight, rubbing it with his hand.

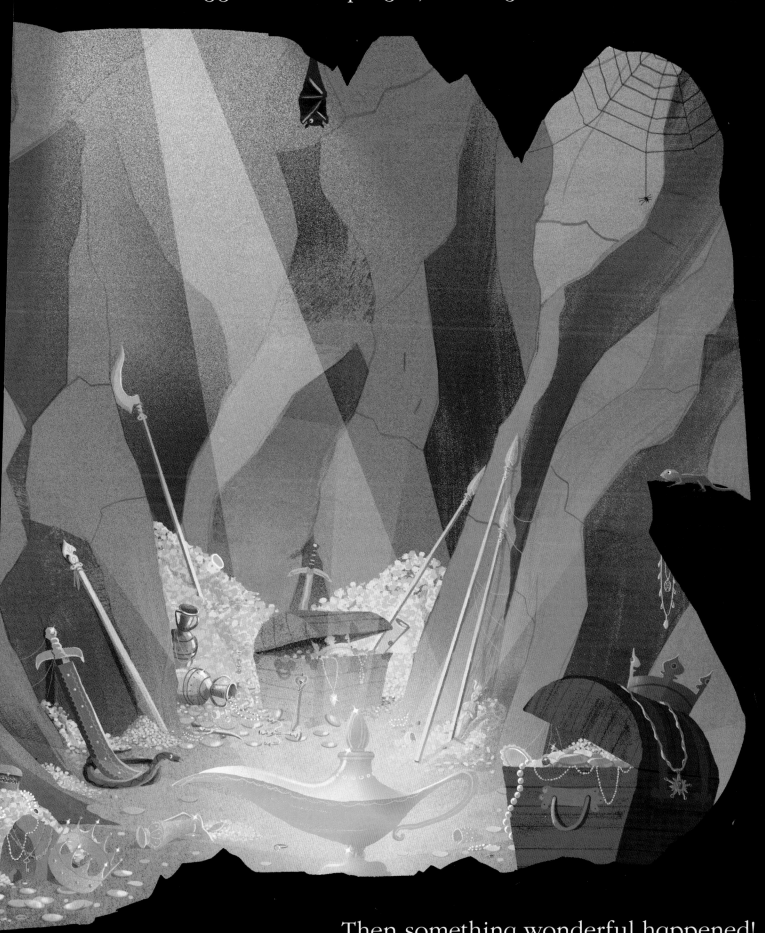

Then something wonderful happened!

A genie appeared from the lamp in a puff of smoke.
"Your wish is my command!" he announced.

Smoke swirled from the genie's fingers. When it cleared, Aladdin was standing in a city street.

Right in front of him was the sultan's daughter, Princess Bala!

"I shouldn't be here," said Aladdin.

"And you *definitely* shouldn't be here."

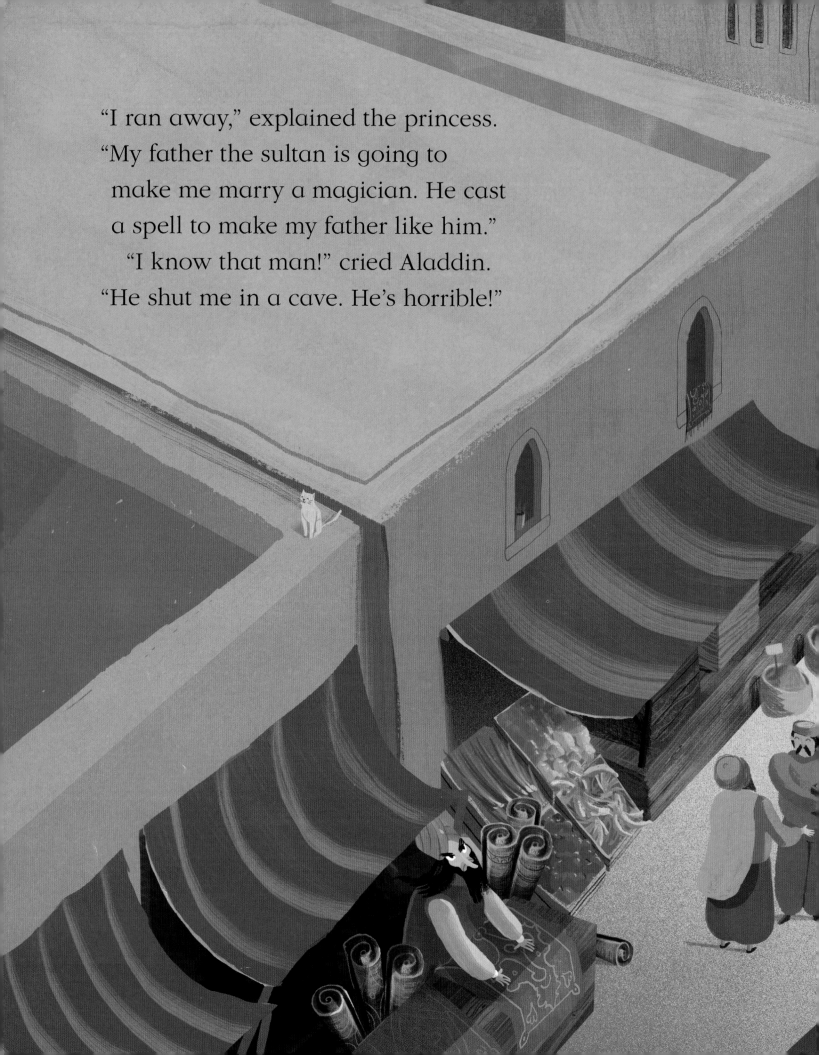

"I ran away," explained the princess.
"My father the sultan is going to
make me marry a magician. He cast
a spell to make my father like him."
"I know that man!" cried Aladdin.
"He shut me in a cave. He's horrible!"

Aladdin and Bala took a magic carpet ride together
far above the city and told each other about their
troubles. Bala said, "Come to the palace tomorrow.
We'll try to reason with my father."

But the next day, as
Aladdin walked to the
palace, the magician
caught him and flung
him into the river.
Aladdin frantically
rubbed the lamp.

"Your wish is my . . ."
began the genie.

Quick! I wish I
was on dry land.

Then the genie said,
"Listen, smartypants, your wish
isn't *always* my command. You
only have three wishes in total."

Meanwhile, inside the palace, the magician was trying everything to make Bala love him.

He gave her flowers.

He wrote her poetry.
(It was awful.)

Finally, he
cast a spell on her.

Aladdin returned and tried to break the spell.
He waved a hand in front of her face. He kissed her cheek.

Then he had an idea. He caught the magician's stinky breath in a bottle and made Bala smell it.

"Urgh!" she cried and went back to normal.

But while Aladdin was helping Bala, the magician snatched the lamp and rubbed it.

"Your wish is . . ." said the genie.

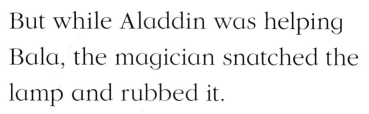

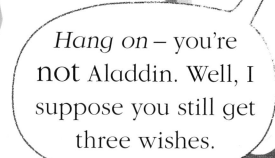

Hang on – you're **not** Aladdin. Well, I suppose you still get three wishes.

The evil man cried, "I wish to be the world's most powerful magician! I wish I was in charge instead of the sultan!"

When the smoke
cleared, they
were all in the
throne room.

"My third wish is to make
Bala love me," said the
magician.

The genie refused!
  "Nuh-uh! I can move stuff
around but I can't force
people to feel things.
Rules are rules."

The magician stamped
and shouted in rage.

Bala crept up behind the magician. But just before she could grab the lamp, he spun around and seized her. He cast a terrible spell. Bala found herself trapped in an hourglass!

"Admit you love me and I'll let you go!" the magician promised.

Never. Ever.

Ever

EVER

EVER!

The magician had
had enough!
"This is all stupid
he cried. "I wish
I was a genie
and didn't have
to bother with
any of you . . .

Oh . . .
        dear . . .
                I just used my final wish!"

The genie was very happy to grant
the magician's third wish. There
was a dramatic swoosh, and
the magician ended up inside
a rather shabby lamp.

When the magician was gone, the
hourglass shattered. Bala was free!

"If only I was a prince then I could
marry you," said Aladdin.
"So use your third wish!" said Bala.
"I can't," Aladdin sighed. "I need
that for something else. Genie,
I wish you were free!"

The delighted genie flowed out of his lamp and disappeared.

Bala turned to the sultan. "See! Aladdin is brave *and* kind. You must let me marry him."

Aladdin and Bala were married that very afternoon. They lived happily ever after – in their very own way.